USBORNE FIRST READING
Level Four

USBORNE FIRST READING
Androcles and the Lion
Retold by Russell Punter
Illustrated by Mike & Carl Gordon

USBORNE FIRST READING
THE EASTER STORY
Retold by Russell Punter
Illustrated by John Joven

USBORNE FIRST READING
The Golden Carpet

USBORNE FIRST READING
The Story of Baby Jesus
Retold by Mary Keily
Illustrated by John Joven

USBORNE FIRST READING
GOLDILOCKS AND THE THREE BEARS
RETOLD BY RUSSELL PUNTER
ILLUSTRATED BY LORENA ALVAREZ

USBORNE FIRST READING
The Magic Wishbone
Retold by Mary Sebag-Montefiore
Illustrated by Qin Leng

USBORNE FIRST READING
The Goose Girl

USBORNE YOUNG READING
The Owl and the Pussy Cat

USBORNE FIRST READING
The Elves and the Shoemaker

The Princess and the Pea

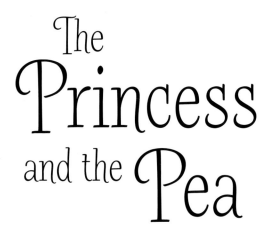

Based on a story by
Hans Christian Andersen

Illustrated by Lorena Alvarez

Retold by Matthew Oldham

Reading consultant: Alison Kelly

There was once a young
prince who loved going
on adventures.

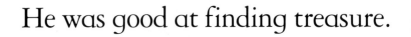

He was good at finding treasure.

He was very good at
rescuing people...

...and he was very, very
good at fighting dragons.

But when the prince came back home, he felt sad.

"I wish I had someone to share my adventures with," he said to himself.

One day, he had an idea...

"I will find someone to marry!" he cried.

He asked his parents for help. They were the king and queen, after all.

I want to get married!

His parents were delighted. "We'll help you find the perfect princess," said the king.

The king and queen
wrote to every princess
in the world. Royal
servants set off
to deliver the
invitations.

Princess Map

PRINCESS
WANTED

Dozens of princesses came to
the palace to meet the prince.
Some came with lots of servants.

10

Some came dripping
with diamonds.

One even came riding
an elephant.

The prince tried to tell them about his adventures, but they were only interested in his treasure.

"They don't seem like *real* princesses to me," he sighed. "Real princesses should want excitement and adventure."

The king and queen
called their best inventors
to a meeting.

"We need a test," the
queen demanded, "to find
a real princess."

14

The inventors tried all sorts
of different tests, but none
of their ideas worked.

Then, one inventor said...

"...I know how to find
a real princess!"

The prince stepped forward.
"How?" he asked.

Two servants pulled back an enormous sheet to reveal a very unusual bed... with a *tower* of mattresses.

"This is the finishing touch,"
said the inventor. She put a
dried pea in the prince's hand.

19

"How will this help?" asked the prince, giving back the pea.

"A real princess notices everything around her," explained the inventor.

"She will be able to feel
this pea through all
these mattresses."

21

The prince invited more
princesses to the palace...

...but none of them
passed his test.

In the morning, each of them declared, "What a comfortable bed!"

The prince felt sad again.

After a while, the princesses
stopped coming. The prince
seemed too hard to please.

PRINCESS
WANTED

The prince gave up hope, too.
He thought he'd never find
someone to marry.

Then, late one night...

KABOOM! Thunder crashed.
Lightning flashed. Rain fell
in big, fat drops.

Through the noise of the storm, the prince heard a thump on the door.

A wet, shivering girl stood on the palace doorstep.

"I was caught in the storm," said the girl. "May I shelter here tonight?"

The girl's sweet voice charmed the prince. He didn't notice her tangled hair or muddy clothes.

"You may stay for as long as you like," said the prince.

Squelch Squelch

As the girl warmed up, the
prince told her all about
his adventures.

The girl listened to every word.

All this talking made the
prince feel sleepy.

Soon, he couldn't keep his
eyes open.

When the prince woke up, he was alone. The girl had gone.

The next morning, the
prince stared gloomily
at his breakfast.

"Why not go on another
adventure?" asked the queen.
"That will cheer you up."

The prince sighed. He didn't
want to go on another
adventure all alone.

Just then, the girl walked in.

The prince jumped up.
"Where have you been?"
he asked.

"After you fell asleep, I looked for a bed," she replied.

"The one I found was very tall. I had to climb in using a ladder."

"Oh?" said the prince, surprised. "How... how did you sleep?"

"Not very well," answered the girl. "I think you need a new bed. That one has a hard lump in the middle."

The king threw up
his hands.

The queen fell
off her chair.

 Ohhh!

The prince's face turned pale,
as he stared at the girl.

"You're a real princess!"
he gasped.

Now the princess looked surprised too. "How did you know?" she asked.

When the prince told her about the pea, the princess started to giggle.

"I've been looking for a real
PRINCE!" she said.

"I've journeyed from palace to palace, looking for a brave prince," the princess explained.

"Everyone has turned me away... except you."

The real prince married
the real princess the very
next day.

The prince and princess never stopped having adventures. They built a museum for all the treasure they found.

In the middle, they put the pea in a beautiful crystal case.

It may still be there today.

About the story

The Princess and the Pea was written by Hans Christian Andersen in 1835. He was born in Denmark in 1805. He left home at fourteen to seek his fortune and became famous all over the world as a writer of fairy tales.

Designed by Laura Nelson
and Sam Whibley
Series Designer: Russell Punter
Edited by Rob Lloyd Jones
Series editor: Lesley Sims

First published in 2017 by Usborne Publishing Ltd.,
Usborne House, 83-85 Saffron Hill, London EC1N 8RT, England.
www.usborne.com Copyright © 2017 Usborne Publishing Ltd.

USBORNE FIRST READING
Level Four

Little Red Riding Hood
Retold by Rob Lloyd Jones
Illustrated by Lorena Alvarez

Why the Sea is Salty
Retold by Rosie Dickins
Illustrated by Sara Rojo

The Town Mouse and the Country Mouse
retold by Susanna Davidson
Illustrated by Jacqueline East

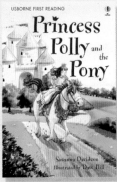

The Emperor and the Nightingale
based on the story by Hans Christian Andersen
Illustrated by Graham Philpot

The Inch Prince
Retold by Russell Punter
Illustrated by Matt Ward

Princess Polly and the Pony
Susanna Davidson
Illustrated by Dave Hill

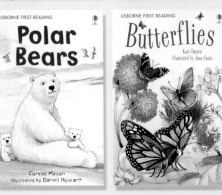

Polar Bears
Conrad Mason
Illustrated by Daniel Howarth

Butterflies
Kate Davies
Illustrated by Jana Costa

Baba Yaga The Flying Witch
Susanna Davidson
Illustrated by Sara Rojo